The Twelve Days of Christmas

PaRragon

Bath · New York · Singapore · Hong Kong · Cologne · Delhi
Melbourne · Amsterdam · Johannesburg · Shenzhen

This Book Belongs To:

charlotte

Illustrated by Caroline Pedler
Retold by Gaby Goldsack

This edition published by Parragon in 2012 for Index Books, Ltd

Parragon
Chartist House
15-17 Trim Street
Bath BA1 1HA, UK
www.parragon.com

Copyright © Parragon Books Ltd 2008

ISBN 978-1-78186-227-8
Printed in China

On the first day of Christmas
my true love gave to me
a partridge in a pear tree.

On the second day of Christmas
my true love gave to me
two turtle doves
and a partridge in a pear tree.

On the third day of Christmas
my true love gave to me
three French hens,
two turtle doves
and a partridge in a pear tree.

On the fourth day of Christmas
my true love gave to me
four calling birds,
three French hens,
two turtle doves
and a partridge in a pear tree.

On the fifth day of Christmas
my true love gave to me
five gold rings,
four calling birds,
three French hens,
two turtle doves
and a partridge in a pear tree.

On the sixth day of Christmas
my true love gave to me
six geese a-laying,
five gold rings,
four calling birds,
three French hens,
two turtle doves
and a partridge in a pear tree.

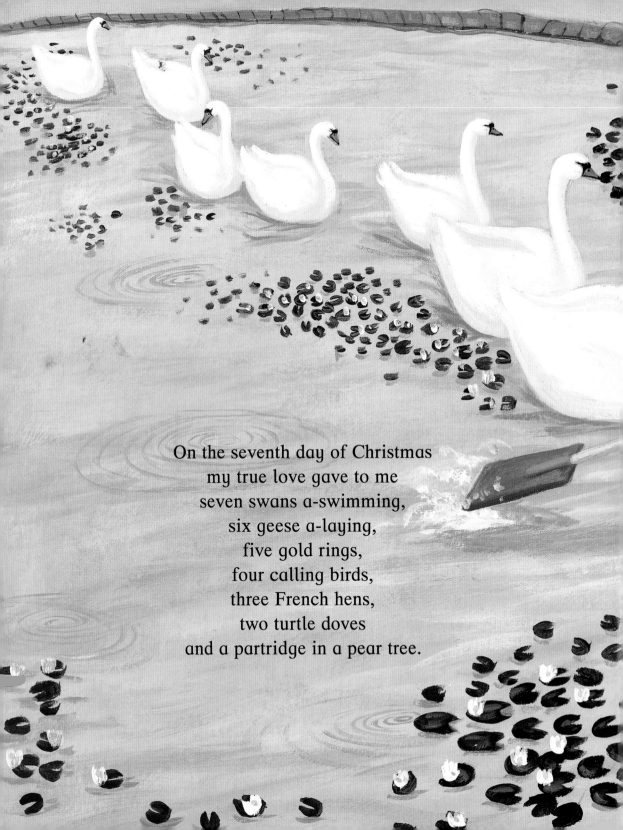

On the seventh day of Christmas
my true love gave to me
seven swans a-swimming,
six geese a-laying,
five gold rings,
four calling birds,
three French hens,
two turtle doves
and a partridge in a pear tree.

On the eighth day of Christmas
my true love gave to me
eight maids a-milking,
seven swans a-swimming,
six geese a-laying,
five gold rings,
four calling birds,
three French hens,
two turtle doves
and a partridge in a pear tree.

On the ninth day of Christmas
my true love gave to me
nine ladies dancing,
eight maids a-milking,
seven swans a-swimming,
six geese a-laying,
five gold rings,
four calling birds,
three French hens,
two turtle doves
and a partridge in a pear tree.

On the tenth day of Christmas
my true love gave to me
ten lords a-leaping,
nine ladies dancing,
eight maids a-milking,
seven swans a-swimming,
six geese a-laying,
five gold rings,
four calling birds,
three French hens,
two turtle doves
and a partridge
in a pear tree.

On the eleventh day of Christmas
my true love gave to me
eleven pipers piping,
ten lords a-leaping,
nine ladies dancing,
eight maids a-milking,
seven swans a-swimming,
six geese a-laying,
five gold rings,
four calling birds,
three French hens,
two turtle doves
and a partridge
in a pear tree.

On the twelfth day of Christmas
my true love gave to me
twelve drummers drumming,
eleven pipers piping,
ten lords a-leaping,
nine ladies dancing,
eight maids a-milking,
seven swans a-swimming,
six geese a-laying,
five gold rings,
four calling birds,
three French hens,
two turtle doves
and a partridge
in a pear tree.